DOODLE'S HOMEWORK

or The Fuddi-duddi-dodo's Great Mathematical Experiment

Story and Pictures by
John Ryan

ANDRE DEUTSCH

British Library Cataloguing in Publication Data

Ryan, John, b.1921
Doodle's homework.
I. Title
823′ .9′ 1J   PZ7.R954

ISBN 0-233-96998-5

First published 1978 by
André Deutsch Limited
105 Great Russell Street London WC1

Printed in Great Britain by
Sackville Press Billericay Ltd

One day on the Island of the Dodos, Doodle, the youngest Dodo, was sitting by the edge of the jungle doing his homework.

It was numbers, and Doodle found numbers very difficult.

"If ONE dodo can eat ONE do-dough-nut . . .

. . . in ONE minute,

how long will it take ONE HUNDRED dodos . . .

. . . to eat ONE HUNDRED do-dough-nuts?

Hm, that's quite a problem!"

Now it happened that the Fuddi-duddi-dodo was taking a little stroll nearby. The Fuddi-duddi-dodo is the oldest bird on the island and is thought to be extremely wise because he wears three pairs of spectacles along his beak and uses very long words. Nobody understands what he is talking about, least of all the Fuddi-duddi-dodo himself, but that doesn't worry anybody.

So Doodle told him what the problem was.
The Fuddi-duddi-dodo looked very wise.

He took a fourth pair of spectacles and put them on.
With three pairs he could see very little. With four he
could see nothing at all.

Then he stood on his head for a while because sometimes his brain seemed to work better that way up. Then he said to Doodle:

Doodle was very puzzled but the Fuddi-duddi-dodo just said: "Never mind, never mind. *I* have just thought of a clever and EASY way of solving this problem. Run away now and play!"

But Doodle didn't run away and play. He wrote down some more figures on his blackboard and then chased after the Fuddi-duddi-dodo calling out:

STOP, *STOP,* MR FUDDI-DUDDI-DODO, *LISTEN* !.. I'VE....

But by this time the Fuddi-duddi-dodo had found his great friend the Presidodo, who ruled the island

and was sitting with his wife, the First Lady-dodo, doing nothing in an important looking way.

And when Doodle arrived out of breath and tried to speak they all looked at him severely, and the Presidodo said:

So Doodle went away.
Then the Fuddi-duddi-dodo explained to the Presidodo all about the problem and about his clever and easy way of solving it. The Presidodo was very excited and cried: "Splendid, splendid! Clearly we shall need help from the Armed Forces. Send for the Brigadodo!"

When the Brigadodo arrived he was very excited, too, and suggested an immediate Council of War. He sent for Lance-Bombadodo Bumble to bring all the things they would need.

Now it happened that the Baddi-dodo was prowling about nearby. The Baddi-dodo spent all his life trying, without much success, to be really bad.

And when he saw what was going on, he thought that his big chance to upset everything had arrived. He listened carefully to the Presidodo

and the Fuddi-duddi-dodo and the Brigadodo, and when at last they had finished making their plans, he made *his* plan, too.

By next morning everything was ready.
One hundred dodos were called early and
sent to the do-dough-nut plantations to pick
one do-dough-nut each and carry it back to
the centre of the island.

Doodle watched. He thought it was all
rather unnecessary. But as everybody was
far too busy to listen to anything *he* said
there wasn't much he could do about it. In
a big open space . . .

. . . the Brigadodo and Bumble were waiting to get them all on parade . . .

. . . for the Fuddi-duddi-dodo's Great Mathematical Experiment.

The Presidodo and his Lady were wearing their
Sunday best,

and the Fuddi-duddi-dodo had set up a special
stop-clock so that he could time exactly how long it
would take for one hundred dodos to eat one
hundred do-dough-nuts. And still nobody paid any
attention to what Doodle was trying to say.

The Baddi-dodo had
hidden himself . . .

. . . in a leafy tree just over the Fuddi-duddi-dodo.
He had a string with a hook on it so that when the
Great Mathematical Experiment started he would be
able to snatch the stop-clock up into the tree and
spoil everything. *Then* people would know how bad
he was!

At last everything was as it should be.

Eager and happy the dodos stood in rows. Each had
a do-dough-nut and all were ready to start eating.

said the
Presidodo,

And the Fuddi-duddi-dodo carried on.

But at that moment . . .

. . . the Baddi-dodo got
so excited and leaned so
far out of his tree that he
fell right out of it and
landed with a THUMP!
. . . on top of the First
Lady-dodo.

The Presidodo ran for his life,

and the First Lady fainted and had to be revived with smelling salts. The Baddi-dodo was arrested, and when at last all was quiet the Fuddi-duddi-dodo had to begin all over again.

They were off! and Doodle daughed like
anything as one hundred dodos . . .

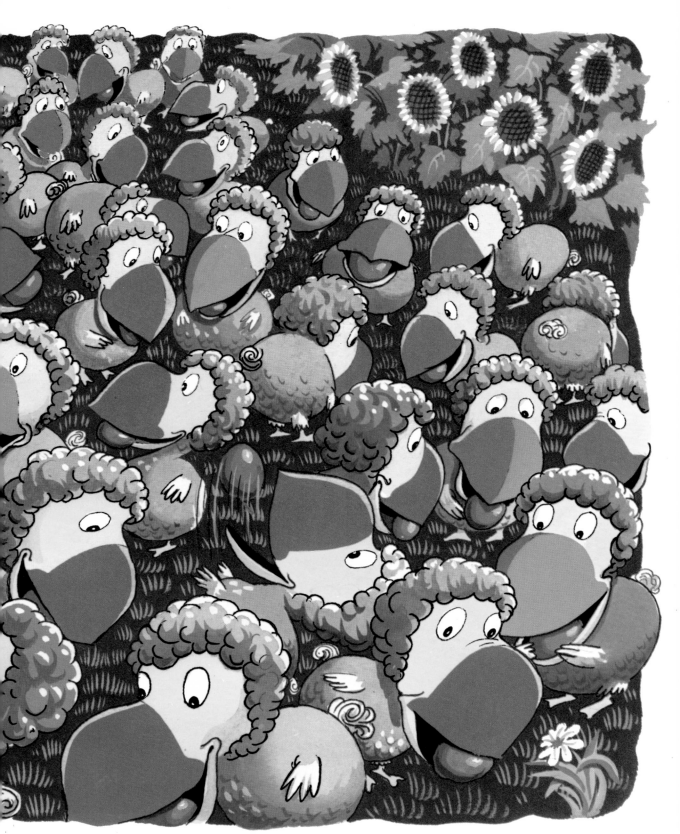

began to gobble and chew at one
hundred do-dough-nuts.

Some of the dodos tried to eat too fast and got indigestion.

But gradually the do-dough-nuts disappeared. There were some ugly moments . . .

. . . when the Baddi-dodo escaped and had to be
re-arrested. And here and there there were quarrels,

but in the end Lance-Bombadodo Bumble was able to
report the end of the experiment.

replied the Fuddi-duddi-dodo,

complained the Presidodo angrily. The Fuddi-duddi-dodo was very upset, but then Doodle called him aside and whispered in his ear: "Here's the answer! I had it all the time!" And the Fuddi-duddi-dodo was saved.

he announced proudly.

And every one of the one hundred dodos cheered and cheered because although none of them understood the Great Experiment, they *had* all enjoyed gobbling up the do-dough-nuts.

The Presidodo felt rather left out of things so he decided to make a speech. But the dodos decided it was lunch-time, and left.

So instead the Presidodo gave the Fuddi-duddi-dodo a medal for being so clever, and the Fuddi-duddi-dodo gave *him* a special fancy hat for his Services to the Advancement of Scientific Knowledge.

Then, feeling very pleased with themselves *they* went home to lunch too. The Baddi-dodo was only locked up for the day. He was furious, because his efforts to be bad had gone wrong as usual.

Nobody paid any attention to Doodle at all. So he went back to his homework.

"It's just as well *I* worked out the answer properly," he thought.

"Though it was a silly question anyway . . .

"*I* could eat *five* do-dough-nuts in *half* a minute!"